Hello, you!

Oh, please don't look

inside of this book.

Turn around and quickly run ...

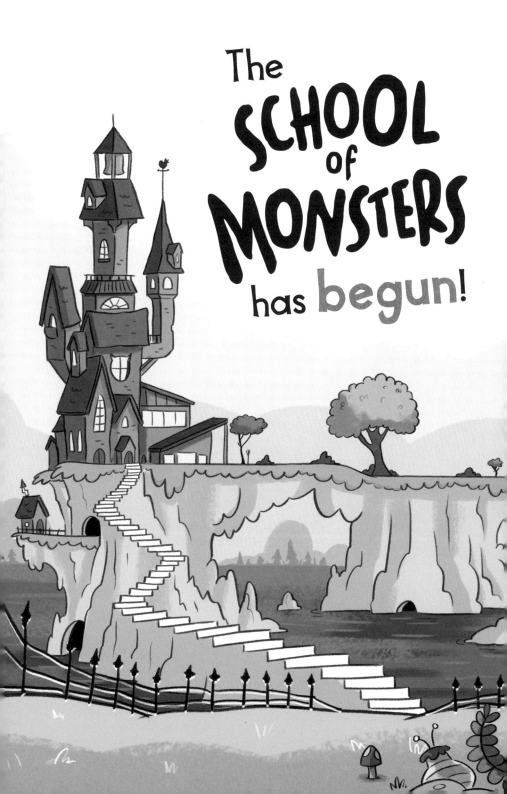

The
SCHOOL
of
MONSTERS
has **begun!**

THIS BOOK BELONGS TO

SCHOOL of MONSTERS

By Sally Rippin

WILLIAM IS A STAR

Art by Chris Kennett

Kane Miller
A DIVISION OF EDC PUBLISHING

Some monsters dance, and some like to **sing**,

but all monsters shine
in at least one **thing**.

Like green monster
William, who's terribly
smart.

He's so good at math,
and he's so good at **art**.

But Will has a secret he's too scared to **say** ...

Will wants to act
in the monster
school **play**.

What you don't know
about William just yet.

is that when he's
nervous he starts
to **fret**.

He wibbles and wobbles
and tugs at his hair.

WIBBLE

WOBBLE

His tummy feels
funny and lets out
some **air**.

SQUEAK!

Will stands onstage, and tries not to **think**

about what they'll
say if he lets out
a stink.

He takes a deep breath
and looks down at his
boot,

but when everyone's quiet, his bottom goes TOOT!

TOOT!

Will jumps up in fright, and he tugs at his **hair**.

But jumping around
only lets out more air.

PARP!

Each time poor Will
stomps his boot on
the ground,

HONK

BLAP

his bottom lets out yet another loud **sound**.

... then Bat-Boy Tim yells, "Hey, William, you rock!

"This play was so boring till you hit the **stage!**"

PLOOF!

"Let's toss out the old one and write a *new* page!"

"Yes!" shout the monsters. "Will, you'll be the **star**!

"You don't need to act. Just be who you **are**.

"We think you're the funniest monster around.

You don't need to speak, let your bum make the **sound**."

POOPH

Two months go by, and the school play has **started**

with William the star of *The Monster Who* Farted.

The tickets sell out. The play is a **winner**!

Now William's top secret is baked beans for **dinner**!

hair
page
ground
say
yet
toot
thing
are
stage
dinner
air
think
started
rock
fret
play
winner
art
farted
star
stink

HOW TO USE THIS BOOK

for adults reading
with children

Welcome to the School of Monsters!

Here are some tips for helping your child learn to read.

At first, your child will be happy just to listen to you read aloud. Reading to your child is a great way for them to associate books with enjoyment and love, as well as to become familiar with language. Talk to them about what is going on in the pictures and ask them questions about what they see. As you read aloud, follow the words with your finger from left to right.

Once your child has started to receive some basic reading instruction, you might like to point out the words in **bold**. Some of these will already be familiar from school. You can assist your child to decode the ones they don't know by sounding out the letters.

As your child's confidence increases, you might like to pause at each word in bold and let your child try to sound it out for themselves. They can then practice the words again using the list at the back of the book.

After some time, your child may feel ready to tackle the whole story themselves. Maybe they can make up their own monster stories, too!

Sally Rippin is one of Australia's best-selling and most-beloved children's authors. She has written over 50 books for children and young adults, and her mantel holds numerous awards for her writing. Best known for her *Billie B. Brown, Hey Jack!* and *Polly and Buster* series, Sally loves to write stories with heart, as well as characters that resonate with children, parents, and teachers alike.

① Using a pencil, start with 2 circles for eyes, eyebrows, and a big smiley mouth.

② Add 3 tufts of hair, some spiky bat-wing ears, and a set of teeth.

③ Now draw curved lines to join the hair and the ears. Add a smiley shape for his chin and a big round tummy.

④ Draw a curved line behind his head for a hat. Use straight lines to make his shorts and sleeves. Then make a curved belt and a triangle tail.

5 Draw on his arms, legs, hands, and boots. Use an eraser to remove the lines on his shorts, if you have one.

6 Time for the extra details! Add collar, buckle, and sleeve lines. Don't forget his pom-pom!

Chris Kennett has been drawing ever since he could hold a pencil (or so his mom says). But professionally, Chris has been creating quirky characters for just over 20 years. He's best known for drawing weird and wonderful creatures from the *Star Wars* universe, but he also loves drawing cute and cuddly monsters – and he hopes you do too!

WELCOME
TO THE

SCHOOL OF MONSTERS

SCHOOL OF MONSTERS
By Sally Rippin
MARY HAS THE BEST PET
Art by Chris Kennett

You shouldn't bring a pet to school.
But Mary's pet is super **cool!**

Have you read ALL the School of Monsters stories?

SCHOOL OF MONSTERS
By Sally Rippin
HAIRY SAM LOVES BREAD AND JAM
Art by Chris Kennett

Sam makes a mess
when he eats **Jam**.
Can he fix it?
Yes, he **can!**

SCHOOL OF MONSTERS
By Sally Rippin
PETE'S BIG FEET
Art by Chris Kennett

Today it's Sports Day
in the **sun**.
But do you think that
Pete can **run?**

Jamie Lee sure likes to **eat**! Today she has a special **treat** ...

When Bat-Boy Tim comes out to **play**, why do others run **away**?

Some monsters are short, and others are **tall**, but Frank is quite clearly the tallest of **all**!

When Will gets nervous, he lets out a **stink**. But what will all his classmates **think**?

All that Jess touches gets gooey and **sticky**. How can she solve a problem so **tricky**?

No one likes to be left **out**. This makes Luna scream and **shout**!

Now that you've learned to read along with Sally Rippin's School of Monsters, meet her other friends!

Hey Jack!

Billie B. Brown

Down-to-earth real-life stories for real-life kids!

Billie B. Brown is brave, brilliant and bold,
and she always has a creative way to save the day!

Jack has a big heart and an even bigger imagination.
He's Billie's best friend, and he'd love to be your friend, too!

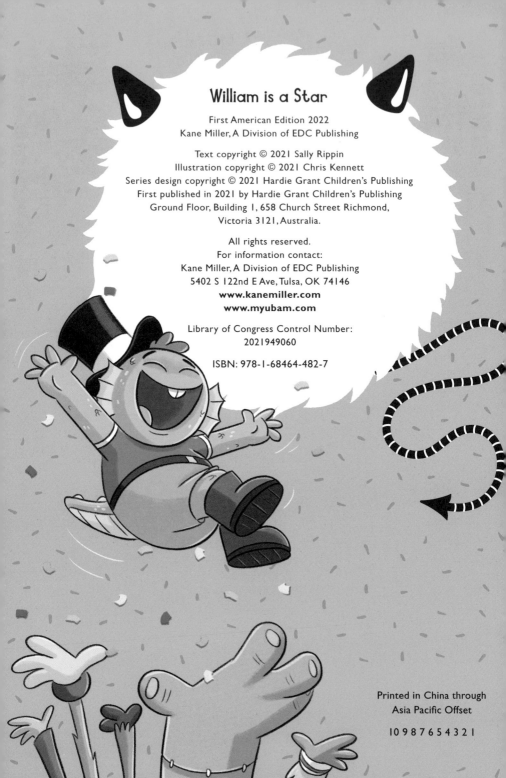

William is a Star

First American Edition 2022
Kane Miller, A Division of EDC Publishing

For information contact:
Kane Miller, A Division of EDC Publishing
5402 S 122nd E Ave, Tulsa, OK 74146
www.kanemiller.com
www.myubam.com

Library of Congress Control Number:
2021949060

ISBN: 978-1-68464-482-7

Printed in China through
Asia Pacific Offset

10 9 8 7 6 5 4 3 2 1